*Illustrations By Izzy King*

"To change the world we must be good to those who cannot repay us."

Pope Francis

This book is dedicated to all the lovers of adventure, who enjoy and wish to preserve the wonders of our shared home.

# Chapter One

**C**umbria is a beautiful county in the North West of England. It is a vast landscape of rolling mountains - known locally as fells – and farmland. The rugged and undulating ground is covered with a mixture of vegetation which thrives on poor soils. You will find striking purple heather or dark green bracken, which looks like a large fern with tough strong roots. Broken rock is found scattered from place to place, dominating the tops of many fells, left by retreating glaciers many thousands of years before. It is an area with peaks and valleys that fill visitors with awe. It is both a place of adventure and retreat.

It had been an unusually warm August day, and a red car turned onto a winding road heading towards a fell that sits between two villages. At three hundred and seventeen metres tall, it is a small fell, the surrounding landscape dotted with mixed tree forests and tarns (which is the northern word for a small lake or large pond).

The car pulled into a lay-by next to the tarn, which sits directly below the fell. The tarn was formed decades earlier, when the beck was damned. Narrow streams from the larger beck, originating high in the fells, still flow into and out of it, with small bridges allowing you to cross.

The engine fell silent, and a door opened. One boot emerged, then another, as Clara stepped out of the driver's seat. Leaping out of the back, two children and a large black dog called Indiana ran from the lay-by along a path that followed the tarn away from the road. Indiana knew exactly where he was. This was one of his favourite walking spots, with no sheep, he was able to run freely wherever he chose.

Clara had walked the route numerous times, and tonight she intended for them all to sleep on the summit. Like most fells, the summit is not visible from below and you must climb to see the top. She was carrying a bigger than usual expedition pack, holding a small tent, three sleeping bags, a bivvy bag, a stove and plenty of food and water. Matthew, was the older of the two children. He was tall for his age and slim with short brown hair. He carried a small pack which had extra food supplies. His sister, Harriet, who was five, not wanting to be any different had her own miniature backpack that was just big enough for a few extra sweets and a carton of apple juice.

Matthew wore long navy combat trousers with a short-sleeved check shirt over his favourite Star Wars t-shirt. Harriet, was running around holding a ball high above her head. Harriet had dark brown hair, like her mother's, but shorter as it was cropped to the shoulder. She wore blue shorts and a t-shirt that said, 'Princess in Training'. She squealed with delight as Indiana ran after her, he desperately wanted the ball she was carrying.

When Matthew and Harriet were younger, Clara had not been out on mountain hikes much, but now the children were at an age where she could be more adventurous again. Henry, their father, had stayed at home whilst he worked and was overseeing important business that had him working long hours. Clara had met Henry on a blind date after she had qualified as a mountain leader. Initially they had become friends sharing a love of travel abroad together. But Matthew and Harriet both shared their mother's passion for the outdoors valuing the sense of freedom it gave them.

As Matthew and Indiana continued to charge ahead through the trees, Clara and Harriet walked steadily behind. Indiana, tired of the ball found a stick and ran back to drop it at Matthew's feet. As usual he obliged the over-excited hound, picking up the stick and throwing it in the tarn. Indiana excitedly leapt into the water and swam after it as if he had never played the game before. Retrieving the stick, he returned to the bank to repeat the process as many times as possible before his human companion tired of the repetition.

The path continued around the tarn, through the trees, until they were on the opposite side to where they had started. The tarn separated them from the car, which was now a small red shape in the distance. The bank of the tarn was lined with trees of varying heights and shades of green. When they reached one of the streams that fed the tarn, Matthew crossed. But as Indiana approached, he jumped in. He bounced along its length towards the tarn, each of his four legs creating big splashes as he ran. When he reached the end of his run, he pounced on the water. He patted the surface with his front paws to create more splashes, which he tried to catch in his mouth.

"Woof -woof!" he barked.

Indiana thought this was the best game ever. He yelped and barked with delight. He repeated the run up and down the stream over and over while Clara, Matthew and Harriet watched, enjoying the fun.

As Matthew moved on ahead, he could see a problem. The herd of Belted Galloway cows, usually found higher up the fell had all congregated on the path that led upwards. Belted Galloways are black furry looking cows with a thick 'belt' of white fur around their middle. They are far more docile than other cattle. As Indiana ran close to one, it just lifted its large head, turning slowly to look at the energetic dog behind it. Unfazed by Indiana's presence, the gentle cow simply returned to munching the grass below.

"Hmm" Clara muttered. She recalled on a previous walk, Indiana had run into a field of Friesian cows, and every member of the herd not only turned their heads towards him, but started moving in his direction. Indiana was much younger at that time and therefore, rather naively, not at all concerned. Clara remembered having to keep shouting at him to come back. Fortunately he did, squeezing back under the gate before any cow had reached him; they had all been heading his way!

Remembering this, Clara worried that if just one of the beasts ahead had a calf or became unnerved by Indiana's presence, then there was no obvious escape. Matthew and Harriet were leaning on the gate posts staring.

"What are we going to do Mum?" asked Matthew.

"We're going to find another way," she replied. "Come on kids," she said turning back.

"Indy!" Matthew called and he ran back squeezing through the fence. He jumped up at him and then onto Clara, who reassured him, rubbing his head.

"Good boy, yes I love you too," she said ignoring the fact he was soaking wet.

From the map, there really was no other footpath, so Clara realised they would have to scale a wall. Dry stone walls are a common feature in the Lake District, acting as field boundaries, they are built without mortar or cement. This means great care would be required to get over one, as the stones can easily shift positions and tumble.

Clara tracked back slowly with Matthew and Harriet now dawdling behind, looking for an obvious point to go over. The walls were tall and the ground in front of them was steep. Clara had to go much further back than she would have liked to find a suitable point. Then a low gap appeared where some stones had fallen. Indiana needed no help to cross, his four legs skipped through the gap. Once over he turned to watch Matthew nimbly climb over the wobbly stones without support, his light but strong frame touching each stone only briefly. Finally Clara supported Harriet on either side of her torso as she climbed to the top of the gap, her short legs a little unsteady on the uneven surface. Matthew reached out to her and clasping his hand, Harriet stepped carefully down. Once safely on the other-side Clara followed.

The field they had entered was thick with shrubs and bracken. As they headed back along the wall, two large horses appeared and watched them intently. The horses were both white with a mottled grey coat. As the four moved on, the horses were obviously curious about the intruders in their field and started to follow. Getting slowly closer, their pace seemed to Clara to have quickened. Neither Clara, nor the children, knew anything about horses, but Clara feared a kick from a horse frightened by Indiana would have serious consequences. So she calmly encouraged Matthew and Harriet to move faster.

However, as they moved more quickly, so did the horses and up ahead another dry-stone wall appeared to block the way. Approaching it, Clara spotted a one metre wooden fence acting as a connection between the wall blocking their way and the other to their right. Indiana, reaching the wall first and realising that they needed to cross, started jumping at various points along the barrier to get over it. Lifting a loose piece of the wooden fence, Clara made a gap big enough for them to get through.

"Come on darling, jump through here," she said to Indiana. "Now you too my love," she said looking at Matthew, who climbed through. "Okay great - now wait and help your sister again please."

Harriet put her right leg through the gap first and sideways on she pushed through with her brother grabbing hold of her right arm and steadying her as Clara on the other side helped lift the rest of her across. "Well done darling, that was brilliant," Clara said as she looked at them both. Harriet was smiling back pleased with herself for accomplishing the task.

"Come on, Mum," urged Matthew, "they're nearly here".

The horses were just a few metres away, as Clara climbed over the wooden fence. The horses kept moving forward as they looked back at them. Reaching the wall, the horses stopped and neighed as if disappointed not to have made contact. The large beasts watched from behind the wall as the intruders disappeared out of their sight. They chatted about their escape as they entered a wooded area.

As the sun began to set the colours of the early evening sky changed around them. The light was fading, and Clara got three head torches out of her pack. Matthew and Harriet put theirs on ready for the approaching darkness. The ground did not yet look familiar to Clara, as they were still a little way from the path. Using the map and compass, Clara worked out the direction they should head in, and, soon enough, they emerged from the thick of the trees to open bracken higher up the fell-side. The familiar stony track re-appeared and now in well-known territory it took another forty minutes, with a quick sugary snack stop to keep the children's spirits up, to near the summit.

Indiana was running this way and that, his nose to the ground like a sniffer dog searching for his prize. He appeared more intensely alive as he ran freely on the fell. As they approached the top, they switched on their torches. As darkness closed in around them, the lights beamed out like a steady stream in front of them with increasing definition. Suddenly, the beams of light emerging from their heads reflected back two large green and shining eyes. There in front of them, on the summit, was one solitary, large, hairy-looking black and white cow.

"What!" exclaimed Clara loudly and rather annoyed.

"Oh wow!" exclaimed Matthew with more of a chuckle.

"Are we going to sleep with a cow tonight, Mummy?" asked Harriet innocently. "No darling - we'd better not," she replied.

They had left the herd by the tarn. How ridiculous, Clara thought, to find one lone cow on the summit! Indiana ran up towards the cow, but it was unmoved by the dog or the disturbance from the head torches.

"Errrggh," Clara sighed. "Come on guys, let's find another spot."

"How far Mummy? I'm tired," Harriet said.

"Yeah, me too," Matthew added, "where will we go now?"

"It's okay, there's another spot very close, just down a little from here." She spoke softly with a reassuring tone.

On the fell there were two cairns, small piles of stones that often mark a route or summit. Sometimes people reached the lower of the two believing it to be the true top. Against the backdrop of an oscillating landscape, and with the line of sight blocked by false peaks, people can be forgiven for thinking this. A great rule of thumb is, if you can see any point higher, then you have not made it.

"We'll head to the lower cairn" she told them. This, she thought, would present another suitable spot. Hopefully this time it would be free from any hooved creatures.

The newly selected area was a small patch of grass surrounded by purple heather growing amongst broken rocks. By nine o'clock Clara had pitched the tent and the two children were snuggled inside their sleeping bags and quickly fell asleep, following the longer-than-planned walk to the campsite.

Clara zipped up the tent and settled in front of it in her own sleeping bag, which was inside a weatherproof bivvy. A bivvy is a lightweight weatherproof covering for sleeping bags. They were first used by climbers who often found themselves sleeping out in rocky areas unable to pitch a tent. They are also ideal for anyone who does not wish to carry a heavy load.

Feeling tired, she rested her head on the rucksack, using it as a pillow. Indiana on the other-hand was not ready to sleep at all and was running around like a lunatic. It was only at four o'clock in the morning he became tired and snuggled into Clara's neck for warmth and comfort.

As dawn broke, the morning light was eerie. A mist had descended in the early hours while they all slept. As Clara opened her eyes, there was no view in any direction and no wind. The only sound was Indiana's excited pant as he presented a stick to the body lying in front of him. Yawning loudly and raising her arms overhead to stretch, Clara ignored Indiana's request and began to formulate a plan of action. The endless mist meant no views and eating a cooked breakfast while watching the sun rise was off the agenda.

It was disappointing. On a clear day the surrounding beauty was breath-taking and unmistakable. The distinct peaks of the Langdale Pikes were visible in one direction, and the vast waters of Coniston Lake in the other. Clara had wanted the children to experience this beauty and discover a love all of their own for the mighty landscape, which was so different from their everyday garden view.

Unzipping the tent, Clara looked in on the two children still snuggled inside their sleeping bags fast asleep. Indiana, pushed past Clara's body to enter and his wet nose nudged Matthews face as he sniffed, causing him to stir.

"Time to get up, my darlings." Clara spoke gently to the now slowly wriggling forms. Indiana decided to turn around stepping on Matthew, his heavy bulk uncomfortable on his small body.

"Indy!" he exclaimed loudly but his voice was muffled by the fabric of the sleeping bag.

"Indy, come out, come on!" commanded Clara. Though excited, the dog obeyed. "Right you two, use the wet wipes to give your faces a good clean and then your body and then get dressed," Clara instructed the bleary eyed pair, who were both now sitting upright looking at her.

"I'll make some porridge for you both, so when you're dressed you can come out and get it. Make sure you put all your layers on - it's not warm."

Matthew and Harriet moved around and chatted inside the tent. Clara sat making their porridge on the camping stove. She looked around and mused. When you reach the top of a mountain, what had looked huge becomes small, and sometimes we could all do with being at the top of a mountain to get that perspective on life. But today the pale morning light was diffused by the tiny droplets of water suspended in the still cold air. Once the two children were dressed and eating their porridge, Clara dismantled the tent and repacked all of their belongings. She told them as they ate to leave no trace of their wild camp. It was important the fells remained unspoiled by human touch, "leave nothing but footprints, and take nothing but photographs."

Once the breakfast things had been collected and packed, they set off slowly. They moved from the steep rocky ground to a grassy track through the bracken. Indiana still full of energy, ran off once more tracking the morning smells of the fellside. Walking in silence, there was nothing remarkable about the three descending the path in the mist, the damp smell in the air and the quietness around them were both familiar until Clara stopped suddenly. The children who had been walking in a daze just behind bumped into her.

About ten metres ahead, there were two large and majestic red deer. The deer were male, as antlers grew like small trees with branches coming out the top of their heads. They stood tall and proud. Their well-defined bodies made them look powerful as they gazed peacefully as if surveying their kingdom. Their red-brown colour contrasted with the backdrop of greyness.

"Magical," Clara muttered quietly under her breath. She had never seen red deer so close before. Matthew and Harriets' eyes widened trying to take in every detail with wonder as they looked on. Frozen to the spot all three watched silently. The deer stood together, without making any sound. Then in unison the two giants moved gracefully, as if they had answered a question in their minds, and disappeared slowly back into the mist.

"Wow!" Matthew said still looking at the now empty spot where they had stood. Harriet started to tug at Clara's jacket and bounce on the spot excitedly.

Clara looked down at them both "Wow indeed - that was a real treat eh?" she said with a sense of excitement.

"Where do you think they went? Can we follow them?" Matthew fired out his questions consecutively.

"Sorry, sweetheart. We could be searching for a long time. We have no idea where they went, and there's no visibility. It's not impossible, but very unlikely we'll see them again."

Matthew's head dropped and Clara added "Hey, don't be discouraged. We've just seen something incredibly beautiful, that many people won't ever get to see." She lowered her body to meet Matthew's face with her own. "Let's smile with the happy memory that's just been made and remember it in our minds eye," she said. "We can't be thrilled every single second of the day, and in life we need to be grateful for every moment – good, bad or ordinary."

"I suppose," he said wearily.

Harriet had been quiet but attentive during the exchange. She looked up at her mother. "But why bad Mummy?"

"Hmm?" Clara responded. She was distracted by Matthew's sullen face. Then she turned her head, "do you mean, why be grateful for bad moments?"

"Yeah," said Harriet emphatically.

"Well, we may not like bad moments, but we can learn from them. They can teach us something new, and that's a reason to be grateful for them."

"Oh," said Harriet thoughtfully.

"Come on, let's get moving, we're driving home to Daddy. He'll love to hear you tell him about this."

"Yay," exclaimed Harriet and she ran a little way ahead before turning round to encourage Matthew. "Come on Matthew - I can't wait to tell Daddy."

Indiana eventually rejoined them, and they all descended steadily back to the point where they had seen the herd of cattle the night before. Not a sign of them could be seen anywhere. With thoughts of getting back home and the adventure, Matthew smiled as they retraced their steps around the tarn and back to the car.

## *Chapter Two*

**C**lara, Matthew, and Harriet had been back from the central Lake District a few days. They had a warm welcome from their father who, despite relishing the quiet time, missed them tremendously. It was a Saturday and that meant that the whole family was home together. It was a hot day with temperatures expected to reach twenty-eight degrees Celsius. All the windows and patio doors were open. Clara was in the kitchen with her friend Rosie, drinking tea and baking treats for the week ahead. The house was often filled with visitors, as they were a social family, open and welcoming. Henry, who also loved to cook, was sitting on the sofa replying to emails on his laptop.

Matthew had his friend Charlie over for the afternoon. Charlie's proper name was Charlotte, but she loved being called Charlie. When asked, Charlie and Matthew would say they had been friends forever. Clara and Rosie, Charlie's mother, were friends before they were born and having given birth not too far apart, they often saw each other for support.

"Did you bivvy out with the children this week?" asked Rosie.

"Not exactly," replied Clara. "I carried a two-person tent with me this time - I just bivvied with the hound."

"I must get out again one day soon," said Rosie, "It's not forecast to rain next week, maybe then."

"Do you remember our first bivvy out on Helvellyn?" asked Clara. She smiled. Helvellyn was the Lake Districts third highest peak over three thousand feet high.

"Of course! How could I forget," replied Rosie.

Clara and Rosie talked about how they had left at dusk to walk over Striding Edge and slept on the summit of Helvellyn. Rosie had initially been afraid of walking across the airy ridge to the summit, but having done it a few times before, this time she took it in her stride. It is a busy route with some walkers taking the lower path around the pointed edges, and then there are those like Clara who thought nothing of scrambling over the exposed top, not worried about the steep slopes to either side.

As the two arrived at the top, they found that sixteen other people had the same idea. Each quadrant of the summit shelter contained four people, and two tents were pitched further away. Clara and Rosie shared their quad with a father and his twelve-year old son. They sat up talking for a while. The father had sourced comfortable bivvy bags from an army surplus store. This had interested Clara and Rosie who only took sleeping bags and large bright orange plastic survival bags to sleep in.

Clara and Rosie remembered the beauty of the sun setting over the mountain tops, and how they dozed off on the rocky ground, their survival bags rustling loudly in a gentle breeze under a blanket of stars. In the morning their giant plastic bags were full of condensation. During the night the sweat from their bodies and the vapour breathed out from their lungs poured into their bright orange plastic cocoons, turning liquid in the cold night air.

"You learn from your mistakes," Clara reflected philosophically. She looked out the window to see Matthew and Charlie running around.

The children were peas in a pod, both loved being active outdoors and adored Star Wars. Charlie's ambition was to explore the world. She was smart and robust, but she did not yet have a career in mind like Matthew who wanted to be a vet. At ten and a half years old, she could be forgiven for that.

The two loved to run around the trees beyond the grass, often tagging each other to be "it". Today Harriet joined them in the garden to play, but Harriet being the smallest and slowest was target more often, she easily tired of the game as she became frustrated at being unable to catch the others. They would get tantalisingly close but then always jump just out of her reach. Harriet, bored and sulking, walked off to the edge of the garden. Leaning up against a tree, she looked across the ground to a sandy patch a metre or so in front of it. There she saw a creature long, grey, and silvery that was basking in the warm summer sunshine. Woah, a snake! She thought and ran off to tell her brother. "Matthew - Matthew," she hollered, "I've found a snake."

"What," replied Matthew, "Where?"

"Over there by the sandy bit," said Harriet, and they all ran over to look.

The slender scaly body slithered a little way along the ground just like a snake would. But it wasn't a snake.

"I've seen one of these before," said Matthew. He lay on the ground on the edge of the sandy depression. "It's not a snake, it's a slow worm," he said.

"A slow worm!" exclaimed Harriet, getting down next to her brother "What's a slow worm?" she asked curiously.

"It's a lizard with no legs," he replied.

"That's so cool," said Charlie bent over and staring at it. She reached out as if to touch it then hesitated "Do they bite?" she asked.

"I don't think so," Matthew said, "but I'm not sure really."

Charlie was bold and quickly but gently had one stroke on the back of its body away from the head before pulling her hand back. "It feels smooth and dry," she said, still staring at it. The lizard was not used to being poked and quickly moved away and disappeared.

They all ran back to tell the story of their encounter and to pick up a much-needed drink. Each emerged back out of the house onto the patio with a cup of orange squash and an ice lolly. They sat on the chairs at first discussing dangerous snakes and then decided to look for the slow worm again. Leaving their lolly sticks and cups, Matthew and Charlie headed back to the sandy area with Harriet running along behind. After a few minutes of looking and picking up sticks to turn over dried out leaves, they gave up and turned their attention to climbing a tree.

The trees in the garden were a mixture of different deciduous species, which means they drop their leaves every winter. One grand old oak had a thick rope hanging from a fat branch about three metres off the ground. Charlie and Matthew had forgotten about Harriet and rushed to climb it in direct competition with each other. Harriet who stood at the bottom, watched them climb up the trunk to the branch with the rope. The two were focussed. They had been up before so showed little fear as one at a time they edged across the branch and then carefully climbed back down the rope.

At the bottom, they heard a cry from above. Harriet, who so wanted to join in and be just like her brother, had somehow climbed up the trunk and was now stuck and afraid.

"What are you doing Harriet?" shouted Matthew, worried he might get into trouble for not watching his little sister more closely.

"I'm stuck!" she shouted back, clinging onto the trunk and sobbing a little.

Matthew instructed Charlie to run up to the house to get someone while he stayed and watched his sister. "It's okay, hold on!" he called up as she continued to sob more openly with tears rolling down her cheeks.

Charlie found Henry in the living room. He sprang up and ran down the garden with Charlie following. Henry was tall and slim. Wearing long shorts, untucked shirt, and brogues, he made quick work climbing up to his daughter. His reassuringly large hands grabbed hold of Harriet, and she released her grip on the trunk and flung her arms around his neck.

"What were you thinking, darling?" he asked gently as he hugged her sobbing body. "It's okay - Daddy's got you now," he repeated softly.

"I'm – I'm sorry Daddy," she mumbled into his chest as the sobbing stopped. "I – I climbed up but – but couldn't come down."

"It's okay, but you are just a bit too small to come up here and be safe," he said.

"I – I just did what Matthew and Charlie did," she said pulling back, her face wet with tears and her red puffy eyes looking into her father's.

"I know," he said gently, "but it's not a good idea to try again - only when you can climb up the rope - then you'll know that you can safely climb down again."

"Okay - I'm sorry Daddy," she said between sniffs.

"It's okay sweetheart, but promise not to try anything again unless Mummy or Daddy are with you," he spoke more firmly this time.

"Okay," she replied nodding her head.

Henry got Harriet to hold on tightly around his neck and grip his body with her short legs as he slowly and carefully climbed back down the trunk. On the ground, Harriet did not want to be put back down, Henry carried her back in his arms to the house.

Matthew decided to avoid the inevitable conversation with both his parents. He and Charlie quickly ran to the garage to get their bikes and head out. As they were about to cycle out of the drive, Clara saw them from the kitchen. "Helmets!" she shouted through an open window.

The two who had their helmets hanging on the handlebars, stopped, put them on and cycled away. Both soon had the wind pressing hard against their faces as they freewheeled down a short steep incline and loved it. The high speed and the sense of freedom were exhilarating. Much better than staying indoors, Matthew and Charlie thought separately, as they flew down the road.

"Where shall we go?" Charlie shouted, as they came to a stop at a small painted roundabout.

"We can't go far. Mum's making dinner and she'll get cross if we're late back," Matthew replied. "Come on, we'll head through the park and loop back and up."

"Cool – let's go!" Charlie said excitedly. Happy and without a care in the world they both pedalled off into the distance.

## *Chapter Three*

***T***he following week Clara and Rosie agreed to meet up. They planned to spend the day out at the zoo with the children for a joint outing. As the red car pulled up outside their house, Charlie's face could be seen watching out for them from the front window. "Mum - James - they're here!" she called. Charlie had blonde hair like her mother. She frequently tied it up in pigtails that stuck out sharply from the back of her head.

Charlie had an older brother called James. He was tall, blonde, and athletic. His passion was for football and the two often tackled each other in the back garden. His superior skill always saw him pass the ball first and more often into the miniature net they had set up to outside.

Clara, Matthew, Harriet, and Indiana entered to a warm welcome from Rosie and Charlie. James was offhand. He did not really like Indiana, who was too excitable and always wanted to get involved with a game of football. As the ball rolled around on the grass, Indiana would land at James' feet eager to take the ball in his teeth. Because of this, they had a designated ball to use when he was about. It was a bit squished where the dog had chomped on it many times. James' prized 'Liverpool' football was safely hidden from view, though somehow he still resented the need to hide it.

Indiana was to stay in the utility room while they were out. He would be walked later, when they returned. The day was again warm in the low twenties. The zoo, which was geared towards younger children, had plenty of ice creams and lollies to choose from in the café.

All the children loved seeing the lions the most. The small pride of females and one male were quite active around midday and also early evening, when the keepers would routinely provide a few meaty chunks. Visitors would hear them roar in anticipation of the drop. It is curious living nearby. When the wind blows in the right direction, the roar of the lions can be heard across the fields and carries into people's back gardens. It is an odd sensation for those who hear their roars, seemingly so close, as they sit eating their evening meal outdoors on the patio.

Returning home after a good afternoon out, Rosie put a couple of pizzas in the oven to feed the hungry hoard, who were now sitting watching James play on his Xbox. Indiana, thrilled at their return, was now out sniffing around the garden, leaving his mark on the odd plant here and there. When the call came for the children to sit at the table for food, Indiana rushed back in and sat patiently next to Harriet who was good at dropping food on the floor. Indiana hoovered up little bits here and there, a useful habit, but once or twice if nothing fell he jumped up placing his paws onto the table surface.

"Get down Indy," Clara would say, and he responded obediently returning to his patient watch.

They left in the early evening, just as Rosie's husband, Phil, arrived home from work. Clara drove just a short distance to walk Indiana, and parked along a lane, tucking the car into a verge to allow other vehicles to pass by. She had packed treats for the hairy hound and the two children to keep them energised. As dusk was not far off, she also had their head torches. She then messaged Henry to let him know where they were and that they would be a maximum of two hours, so he could eat if home before them.

They set off walking down the lane towards a church and farm. Indiana was on the lead for a few good reasons. Firstly, his tendency to explore led him into front gardens. On one occasion he went through a dog flap into a stranger's home! Secondly, though the footpath only took them around and not through the farm, there were free range chickens about, and Clara did not trust the wolf in him to not chase them and maybe worse.

The footpath led through the churchyard. The church was a thirteenth century building and being Grade I listed was well maintained. The gravestones around it however were covered in lichen and overgrown ivy. Looking closely at the writing, the tombstones all dated to the nineteenth century, and were hard to read with the biological damage and weathering they had endured over the last hundred plus years.

Leaving the Church, the path opened out and skirted around a large yard owned by the farm. To their right was an old mill house, only identifiable by the giant wheel attached to its side that guarded the main entrance to the farmer's property. The open land behind it had a large, tarmacked area surrounded by grass. Parked on the grass, there were old shabby-looking steam engines, that had perhaps been purchased for refurbishment. On a large trailer there was a long white boat. A giant green tarpaulin covered the top of the boat, so you couldn't see its condition.

The four turned left and Indiana was released to run free along the field ahead. As they walked, llamas were eating from a hay bale in the fenced-off field to their right. The animals looked up and started trotting purposefully closer towards them. The sun was lowering in the sky and its long golden beams shone out across the field behind the llamas. As Matthew and Harriet approached the fence, two llamas stood on the other side towering above them. One, a dark tan, appeared to be looking away but had one eye focussed on Indiana. The other, a soft golden colour, had its head lowered looking at the two children.

"Wow, she's big eh," Clara said reaching out to stroke her nose. Initially the llama lifted its head away from her hand. "It's okay," she soothed and slowly let the llama sniff her hand, before then being allowed to stroke its head. "See – they're social animals," she said, smiling.

Indiana, seeing the attention being given to the llamas, ran over jealous. He jumped up at Clara, who was still stroking the large animal. She turned to Indiana, reassuring him that he was the best dog ever and her favourite animal. Matthew was next to stroke the llama, but Harriet was too small to reach up high enough and so just held out her hand, hoping the beast would bend down far enough for her to touch. Indiana moved closer to the llama, clearly nervous. As the llama bent lower to look at him, the dog jumped back a little, then edged closer again. Eventually for a few seconds the two sniffed each other before Indiana retreated and started to whine. It was if he was saying 'that's enough now – let's go.'

Harriet waved goodbye to the llamas, who continued watching their departure with interest. The family came to the end of the field and turned down another short track to a large iron gate that marked the start of a footpath through a small patch of woodland. As they followed the path through the trees, there were leaves underfoot, which had fallen in winter and dried out in the summer heat. Indiana ran at full speed leaping over fallen branches towards the river that flowed further ahead. The river meandered through flat farmland. It was narrow with steep banks, until it opened out and widened a mile or so further on. They had walked that far before and seen the two resident swans that hissed at Indiana, when they thought he had come uncomfortably close. Sensibly Indiana made no attempt to go after them and left them to paddle silently along in peace.

After Indiana had splashed around for a while, with the children standing above him on the bridge throwing twigs down onto the water, it was time to move on. The light was nearly gone from the late evening sky. The golden sun had disappeared below the horizon, leaving a clear inky blue sky above and a large full moon rising up into it.

"Where is the moon when it's day Mummy?" asked Harriet.

"Good question lovely, it's still there, but the earth is always turning, so the sun rises and sets, and so does the moon," replied Clara.

They headed back crossing styles, through more fields, until in darkness, they were back in the same field by the farmyard and the church. Indiana was put back on his lead and they walked along, with their head torches beaming out. Before leaving the field, Clara suggested they turn off the lights to see how bright it was with the full moon, which was now higher in the sky. The pale silvery light was very bright indeed and they observed their moon shadow with delight. Clara told them, that in the olden days before the invention of torches, robbers would wait for a full moon and use its light to steal and commit crimes in the night.

"Okay, head lights back on - let's go!" she finished. With that thought still in their heads they turned and could see the shapes of the rusty trains ahead. All gazing forward, they all saw a shadowy figure glide across the white hull of the boat. But there was something different about its movement, and something just generally odd about its appearance. They saw the shadow but no physical body to form the shadow had passed by it. The shadow had also moved quickly, but not bobbing up and down as a runner would. It glided as if stood on something else moving below them. But there was no noise, nothing mechanical was around to have caused what now could only be called an apparition.

Matthew stopped, stunned. All his brain cells were working to interpret what he had never seen before and could not explain. His face had a blank expression, and he was not sure how to react or feel about what he had seen. His head snapped back to look at his mother's face for clues about how he was meant to respond. Clara was fascinated.

"What was that?" Matthew asked looking back to where the moving shadowy figure had been. With no obvious explanation, Clara responded saying she did not know, and perhaps it was someone doing a job late in the dark. Matthew was suspicious and wanting to test his mother's hypothesis, he ran forward into the yard and shouted "hello." No reply came.

"Mum – there's no-one there," he ran back to announce. As they continued forward, there wasn't a sight or sound of anyone else.

"It disappeared, Mummy," Harriet added.

"It was a ghost!" exclaimed Matthew.

"Maybe," Clara conceded.

"What's a ghost Mummy?" asked Harriet.

"Ooh, I don't think anyone knows darling - Aunt Jane says they're shadows from the past," she said thoughtfully.

"It's really spooky!" said Matthew.

"Yes, it is, let's get ourselves back to the car!" replied Clara.

They got to the opening of the churchyard and walked through together. Matthew was looking intently in all directions wondering if his light would reveal another shadow of the past hiding between the gravestones. Clara and Harriet were also looking about for the same reason. Perhaps, they wondered, it was the bright light of the moon tricking their eyes in the darkness. But the four arrived at the wooden gate that led them out and they continued uneventfully back along the lane and to the car.

## *Chapter Four*

**L**ate morning on the following day, Clara, Matthew, Harriet, and Indiana rang the bell of Aunt Jane's front door. She opened the door with a big smile, "Hello! Come on in," said Aunt Jane.

Matthew and Harriet stepped forward into a warm embrace, one under each arm. Aunt Jane was a typical member of Henry's family, being tall and slim. She was Henry's aunt, active and full of life for her older age.

Indiana jumped up to greet Aunt Jane, but Clara pulled him back down.

"No Indy – no jumping up," she said with a slightly frustrated edge. Jumping up on people was the one thing she had not been able to train him not to do.

"Hello Indiana!" Aunt Jane said smiling and bending to stroke his head.

"I'll just go and put the kettle on – tea and orange juice okay?" asked Aunt Jane.

"Yes please, thank you," said Harriet following her brother.

Matthew and Harriet headed outside to a small back yard, which opened out to the sea. Indiana followed Clara and Aunt Jane into the kitchen.

"Indiana looks bigger, every time I see him," remarked Aunt Jane.

Clara recalled when Aunt Jane had accompanied her to the farm where Indiana, was a puppy for sale. Clara really wanted a dog and specifically the clever and gentle Labrador Border Collie cross.

When they arrived there were only two puppies left. Clara had immediately known which puppy was for her, as they stood talking to the farmer's wife. One was hidden shyly behind the wife's legs. The second on the other-hand, came running out of the house straight up to Clara, grabbed her handbag in his mouth and ran off with it.

"That's the one," said Clara with delight.

"Oh, how funny is that!" declared the farmer's wife. "So you're going for the naughty one?" She laughed.

"Well, he's certainly got character," Clara responded cheerfully.

When Indiana had been brought back to Aunt Jane's house, Aunt Jane stayed with him while Clara headed out to get dog supplies. She returned with food, bedding and toys, and opened the door to a frantic looking Aunt Jane who exclaimed "thank goodness you're back! He's into everything! I've tried to put everything out of reach, but he just hasn't stopped!"

"Oh, Matthew and Harriet are going to love him!" Clara said excitedly.

Even as a young pup, Indiana was strong, pulling hard on the lead, and had the habit of jumping up to greet people with enthusiasm. Aunt Jane recalled to her dismay how Indiana, having covered himself in mud, jumped up onto an unsuspecting man while they were up a small hill close to the town. Indiana's muddy paws left the man, who had unfortunately been wearing a cream suit, splattered with mud and very angry. Indiana on the other-hand looked extremely happy and ran off to continue the walk. Clara laughed as they moved to sit outside remembering that they too decided that running away at that point was a good idea.

"Ahh, funny memories," said Aunt Jane in her thick Cumbrian accent.

"And how are you, Matthew?" asked Aunt Jane.

"Yeah, great thanks – we saw a ghost yesterday," he told her eager to share his story.

"Oh, really!" said Aunt Jane surprised, "tell me what happened Matthew, I like a good story."

She sat back into a deck chair, her silver hair and blue and white clothing complimenting perfectly the blue and white stripes of the chair. Matthew went onto recount the tale of the walk and the moving ghostly shadow. He covered all the possible reasons for what they had seen and discounted them with the observed evidence just like a true detective.

"Oh my, that is a fascinating tale Matthew," she said delighted by the novelty of their conversation.

"You know – I had a ghostly experience once, many years ago now – it was quite extraordinary." Her voice was gentle but wobbly with her age.

"Oh really - please tell us," Matthew asked.

Harriet picked up a cup of orange juice and settled next to her brother, "what is a ghost?" she asked looking at Aunt Jane.

"Oh, well now, some people think they're lost souls, looking for treasure left behind in their past life – but they never find it, of course, because the real treasure is love, that is the greatest treasure and they just didn't live their life filling themselves up with enough love," she replied.

"Now," she started, a slight glimmer in her eye as she became excited about telling her own story. "It happened before I met my late husband, your uncle Joe – I went to Scotland and stayed in a bed and breakfast one night, in a small village not too far from Inverness. The owners, a lovely couple, when checking me in said that should I need anything, or have any trouble in the night, I should not hesitate to wake them up. Later, I was sat up in bed with the television on and finishing off writing in my journal. Just as I had put it down, the lights and the television flickered on and off a couple of times. I thought the power was about to go out, but then it stopped, came back on and all seemed fine, so I thought nothing of it. I remember picking up a glass of water off the table beside me before getting up to switch the television off, and the room just all of a sudden became freezing cold."

As she spoke, her face had become serious, and a faraway look was in her eyes as if seeing it all happen again in her mind's eye. They sat gripped listening attentively, eyes unmoving from her face as they absorbed her every word.

She went on, "then the wardrobe beside the television started to shake, I thought it was an earthquake until I realised that it was only the wardrobe moving and nothing else in the room. By now of course, I was terrified, then the wardrobe doors flung open, and I remember screaming. The wardrobe doors were heavy you see, they were mirrored, I couldn't think of anything other than the supernatural that could do such a thing. So terrified I dropped the glass, jumped out of the bed and ran out of the room, and called for the owners to come at once."

"What did they do?" Matthew asked.

"Well, they'd had trouble before, and immediately called the local vicar to come as he'd promised to help if this ghost turned up again."

"Did he not mind being called so late?" Clara asked.

"Well, no, he wanted to help – Father Green he was called. When he arrived, he held a large cross in one hand opening the door with the other, and no sooner had he done that – well – a blast of cold air rushed into the hallway. So he held up the cross, saying words I'll never forget, "visit this house, we pray Lord, drive away the enemy, bring your holy angels and send your blessings and peace upon this place." And as he spoke the light bulb in the room glowed brighter and brighter, until it seemed as bright as the sun, then another rush of wind came from behind us going into the room, and the light bulb popped! An explosion of glass pieces shattering and falling on the floor. But it worked! The cold was gone. The Father turned to us in the hall and said, 'when you need it, help is never far away.'"

"Wow!" said Matthew.

"Yes, that is an extraordinary story!" said Clara.

"Right! Well, now it's about time for a walk along the beach I think, don't you?" said Aunt Jane with enthusiasm. They got up and headed for a small gate at the back of the garden.

The beach was a mix of terrain that started with grassy plants furthest from the sea and gave way to pebbles. Golden sand was revealed when the tide was low, interspersed with a few rocky outcrops.

Clara watched as the two children played with the excited hound. They took turns throwing the ball, followed by a long attempt to get it back from the dog. There were shouts of "drop! - drop! - drop it Indy!" then they would run a short way followed by the dog with his eyes fixed on the hand that carried the ball. If a hand dropped low, the dog's head lowered and if they raised it up, his head went high. Indiana wanted the ball, and he wanted it badly. When the ball was flung in the air, Indiana leapt after it every time with such vigour and never seemed to tire of the highly repetitive game.

As Clara and Aunt Jane walked slowly looking out over the sea towards the silhouette of a small island in the distance, excited cries were suddenly carried by the breeze. The two women looked over immediately.

"Mum! – Mum! There's a crab here." "We've found a crab!"

Clara and Aunt Jane went over to where Matthew and Harriet were bent over, studying their find. Indiana also ran swiftly to inspect, his interest sparked by the enthusiasm of the cries and Clara's movement.

"It's a crab Indy," cried Harriet excitedly as he arrived at the scene.

Indiana stepped closer to the moving crab, which was suddenly in the shadow of the large beast. Indiana bent down to sniff the creature. It had been moving sideways, but now stopped to raise its large pincers in the air ready to defend against a possible attack.

"No Indy!" Yelled Matthew, "watch your nose!"

"No Indy, no!" Echoed Harriet, sounding worried.

Indiana continued sniffing close to the small crustacean and the crab began swiping its pincers in the air above its head. Clara arrived and grabbed Indiana's collar and pulled him away.

"You'll get pinched Indy," Clara said in a gentle voice, but gripping his collar firmly.

"What type of crab is it, Mum?" asked Matthew.

"No idea, Matthew," she replied, crouching down for a closer look. "Remind me to look it up later."

"Okay," he agreed. Matthew loved animals and wanted to learn all he could about the natural world. He had a particular fascination with sea creatures. He had posters of dolphins, whales and sharks on his bedroom wall back home.

Indiana's removal, brought the sunshine back to the crab who, sensing the change, continued its journey to a small pool of salty water by the underside of a rock. Here they watched as it shuffled backwards into the sand and disappeared from sight and to safety.

"That was fun!" remarked Clara who stood up straight and let Indiana go. "Well you two, we should head back to the house and get ready to go."

Leaving the house, Matthew and Harriet simultaneously hugged Aunt Jane who bent over them with her arms widely embracing them both.

"Thank you for having us, Aunt Jane," said Matthew.

"Yes, thank you Aunt Jane," said Harriet.

"Aww, you're welcome you two - you both be good now." Aunt Jane let go of them.

"We will," Matthew replied as he got into the car.

Harriet skipped off after her brother and climbed in the other side, before she too shouted "we will," again mimicking her brother.

Smiling, Clara and Aunt Jane said their goodbyes and once all were secured, and Indiana closed in the back, the engine started, and the red car disappeared along the road.

## *Chapter Five*

***A*** few days later and not much after midday, the red car turned onto a road heading up a steep hill, towards a little village. The engine whirred as the vehicle chugged its way up the steep road until it came to a plateau and turned into a small carpark amongst the trees. One green welly emerged, then another, as Clara stepped out of the car.

Although it was warm Harriet had insisted on wearing her blue wellies and her mother had to wear hers too. Matthew, who let himself out by climbing over to the driver's seat and leaving by the same door as his mother, was not having any of it. He, sensibly he thought, wore his trainers. Matthew ran around to the back and opened the boot. Indiana leapt excitedly from the car, his tail wagging furiously as he took in the new surroundings. Kings Wood was another of his favourite walking spots, an ancient woodland, filled with a variety of animals, plants and fungi.

The two ran off into the woods, Matthew loudly charging ahead. Clara picked up her day pack and locked the car. Harriet skipped by her side as they also entered the woods. Indiana was rushing about from tree to tree investigating new smells as he went. The sun rays came through the trees like fingers pointing from the sky and a gentle breeze pushed the leaves this way and that, producing a soft calming rustle from the canopy above.

The trees closed in around them as they went deeper into the woods. Ahead of the others, Matthew stopped to look back and, in that moment, noticed a strange sound, one he had not heard before. It was a strange rustle that was not of the wind. Looking around, his gaze fell to the forest floor, and his eyes followed from his feet across to a giant ant's nest.

The nest was about one foot tall and made of dead pine needles and twigs. The sound was that of a thousand wood ants crawling through the tinder dry leaf litter. 'Awesome' thought Matthew, who searched for a stick to poke around the marching ants. Looking more closely he saw some of the large ants co-ordinating the movement of a dead beetle across the ground.

"Mum – Mum," he called. "Look at this."

Harriet arrived first as she started running to where he was. Matthew pointed the stick and beckoned her to look closely to see the beetle.

"Yuck," she shrieked when she realised what he was looking at. Clara caught up and also looked closely.

"Wow – that's amazing – I haven't seen such a big nest before," she said.

"And they've got a beetle Mummy," said Harriet, Matthew helpfully pointing it out with the stick.

"Oh yes! I see it – they're worker ants carrying food to the nest."

"Food for all the other workers?" Matthew said thinking out loud.

"Hmm, maybe - but likely to feed the queen who'll be busy laying her eggs," Clara said.

"The queen?" Matthew repeated with a quizzical face.

"Yep." Clara smiled and went onto explain that the queen would be in the rather hot middle of the nest, the biggest of all the ants, but aggressively defended by her workers. "These ants have strong jaws that'll nip you if you get too close," she said.

"Eeek," Harriet shrieked again, dancing about in her wellies to be sure none would get her.

"Come on, darlings. We'd better not stay here too long." She carried on ahead with Harriet jumping about in a Tigger-like fashion beside her.

Indiana, who was out of their sight, was still racing around, left to right, backwards and forwards sniffing the ground as he went. Then he stopped. Something had his attention, a new smell. His head lowered, and sniffing quickly, he followed the ground slowly into a patch of longer grass.

"Woof - woof," he barked. His nose had landed on something prickly and the prickly object was moving.

Matthew who had not moved and was still poking leaves about the ants heard Indiana barking and immediately turned and ran to find out what was going on. "Woof - woof," he continued. It was not a creature he had seen before. The small prickly creature seeing Indiana became frightened and curled up tightly into a ball.

"Woof – woof," he carried on barking. Clara, Matthew and Harriet quickly caught up and laughed when they saw what he had found.

"It's a hedgehog, Indy," Matthew chuckled.

"It's okay, silly," Harriet said, while Clara pulled Indiana away from the hedgehog. Harriet moved to stand next to her brother, then started to creep closer to the spiky ball.

Matthew grabbed her arm. "No, wait," he said, "it's scared – we need to stay quiet."

"But I want to see it," insisted Harriet whispering now.

"Gosh, it's really upset you," Clara said, dropping to her knees to stroke and comfort Indiana. "Did the hedgehog prickle your nose - aw - bad hedgehog!" She reassured him in a soothing voice. Matthew looked back at his Mum with a big beaming smile, but Harriet's eyes were fixed on the creature.

Slowly it uncurled to reveal a long hairy snout, with a black button nose and tiny black eyes. Harriet's eyes grew bigger and her face lit up. She watched it begin to go back to the business of foraging for juicy slugs. But the hedgehog sensed the location was compromised and it waddled speedily into the deep shade of the surrounding tall shrubs. They were thick with brambles entwined in grass and dead leaves fallen the winter before.

As they continued on, they arrived at a tree-lined bridleway. Indiana, charging about looking for the next thrill, spotted a large muddy puddle and 'splosh' he was in. Mud! Lovely mud! Indiana lapped up the muddy water and then 'splat' he laid down and rolled in it until he was covered head to tail.

"Errrghhh!" Clara and Matthew exclaimed almost simultaneously.

Indiana was so happy, his tail wagged furiously from side to side as he stood up. As Clara passed by, Indiana jumped out, ran a little way ahead and stopped.

"Uh Oh" Clara said out loud as she knew what he was about to do, and yes there it was, Indiana shook himself vigorously from side to side, his ears flapping up and down. The mud splatter fired off in all directions. The children screamed and laughed, as they ran away from him.

"Thanks, Indiana!" Clara said as she held her hands out in front of herself to block the mud spray from reaching her clean clothes. Indiana looked back and barked with delight, before running ahead he turned right to head once more into the trees. Then Indiana caught the scent of something small and grey, a creature with fur and a long bushy tail. Then he saw it. Indiana sped off panting hard and jumping over fallen branches and shrubs to catch up. But the squirrel had heard him coming and already started to climb a nearby tree. Indiana stopped at the tree, looked up and watched as the grey squirrel skilfully jumped from one branch to another and was gone.

Suddenly over the brow ahead, a man approached on his bike. Kings Wood has a variety of undulating and rough tracks making it an ideal challenge for mountain bikers. The cyclist yelled out "do you have a Labrador?"

"Yes," Clara replied.

"He's up ahead just to your right," he shouted, as he whizzed past and disappeared quickly.

"Thanks," Clara called back smiling. Clara whistled for Indiana and a few moments later there he was galloping back towards her, his tongue hanging out one side of his mouth.

They all climbed slowly up a steep bank and into the shady darkness of more trees. Matthew picked up a stick and ran after Indiana who once again was ahead. "Aaaaargghhhhhh" he screamed as he ran with his arm outstretched and the stick bashing the trunks of trees that he passed. Harriet excited by her brother's charge, grabbed her own stick and did exactly the same but much more slowly. She let out a high-pitched squeal and deliberately tapped the trees, as she went.

They followed the path along to a large man-made pond and Indiana with a big splash was in. 'Splish, splash' Indiana's paws patted the water and he barked with excitement as he tried to catch the splashes in his mouth. Then jumping in deep, he swam around in circles, making waves and whining with delight. Whenever Indiana reached the end of the pond, he turned back, sharply creating even bigger waves as his body came up out of the water and then crashed back down. Matthew threw a stick into the water, which Indiana collected and brought back. After ten minutes of play Indiana jumped out and shook off. He then went to a grassy patch where he dropped, rolled and wriggled about to get more of the water out of his fur.

The three laughed as he writhed about on the grass. Matthew was closest and spotted something unusual on the grass.

"Mum!" He called.

Clara and Harriet moved to look where Matthew was pointing. There on the ground was the severed hoof of a deer. Harriet pulled a face, as Clara inspected the find more closely. It was about twenty centimetres long and was in fact the lower part of a deer's leg with the hoof intact. The skin was still on most of it, but looked cleanly cut. The edge was the same level all the way around the leg bone that protruded out the middle. The white bone was slightly pink inside, and the severed limb looked fresh.

"Oh - well – that's not nice," Clara commented.

"What's it doing here?" asked Matthew, "where's the rest of the deer?" he persisted.

"No Indy – no," said Harriet as the dog moved closer to sniff.

"I don't know," replied Clara. She knew there were foxes about that could easily have moved the severed hoof away from where the unfortunate deer had fallen. But what concerned her more was the perfect edge of the skin around the bone. Could it have been caught by a poacher? Could a poacher be using a snare? Are there snares about that could harm Indiana? The questions plagued her and she decided the hoof needed to be reported and investigated. When she explained to the children, Matthew asked what a snare was. Clara told him that they were wire loops used to trap animals, causing great suffering. They are illegal and it would be a criminal offence to use one in this country.

Clara took a spare plastic bag out of her rucksack. She always carried one to pick up rubbish. You have a responsibility she always said to the children, to not walk past rubbish, thinking how terrible it was someone had dropped it to then just leave it there. Inaction following a judgement of someone else, she thought, made you just as guilty as the thoughtless person who dropped it.

Using the bag as a glove, she picked up the hoof and folded the bag down around it. It didn't smell fresh, but then who knows what creatures could have gnawed on it. She put the package into a mesh side pocket on the outside of her pack.

"Come on kids - we're going to report this."

## *Chapter Six*

***I***t had been another roasting hot day. After they arrived home from a food shop, Matthew had spent an hour helping tidy up, before they all had some tea. Now, early evening, Matthew was in the kitchen with his mother, waiting for his friends to arrive. The tent they would all sleep in was brought out of the cupboard and was in the hallway ready to pitch after dinner. Clara was preparing a spaghetti Bolognese to feed the hungry mouths. The meat sauce was simmering gently on the stove and the dried pasta left on the side ready to cook once all had arrived.

Indiana was stretched out asleep in the shade under the patio table outdoors. Harriet had left the two in the kitchen and was back out in the garden. She was an imaginative and enthusiastic free spirit, who loved exploring the bottom of the garden. In her mind it was the perfect place for fairy tales. She liked to place her soft toys in different places and tell them these spots would be great for an adventure. Clara and Henry watched Harriet talking to herself in the garden, Clara would tell Henry how like Harriet she was when she was small.

Harriet headed towards the edge of the garden and the start of the private wooded area, but then she stopped. About five metres in front and just behind the wire fence, she could see a badger. The black-and-white animal looked young. It was smaller than some she had seen before. It did not notice Harriet. She started moving slowly closer as it rummaged through leaf litter looking for tasty slugs to eat. It must be hungry, Harriet thought as she got closer. It was so focussed on turning over the leaves, the rustling must have masked her footsteps. She was less than a metre away, and could not believe how close she was to this beautiful creature. Suddenly the badger stopped its search, and looked up. Startled by Harriet's looming presence, it turned sharply and ran as fast as it could to get away. She thought how funny badgers look when they run, their large bodies and short legs bouncing up and down. The badger, now about ten metres away, stopped and looked back before bouncing off into the distance.

Harriet was excited and ran back to the house to tell her mother and brother about her amazing encounter. As she told her tale, Charlie arrived with her mother, Rosie, and her brother, James. Charlie and Matthew ran off upstairs to Matthew's room, leaving Clara and Rosie chatting in the kitchen. Harriet took James outside to show him where the badger had been. Soon after Charlie's arrival, Sebastian also arrived with his mother Harper. Sebastian was the same age as Matthew and went to the same secondary school. They had met, not just because they were in the same year group, but also in the same tutor group. Charlie had started year seven at an all-girls grammar school, something she disliked immensely, which consequently meant she did not know Sebastian at all well.

Matthew and Charlie ran back downstairs to meet the new arrivals and they all stayed and chatted in the kitchen. Clara offered to feed everyone, but Rosie had to leave for an appointment and went to find James. Harper wanted to be back home to greet her husband, Mark. They were looking forward to a date night and the house to themselves.

As afternoon turned to early evening, Henry arrived home and they all sat eating outdoors on the patio.

"Can we get the fire going tonight, Dad?" asked Matthew.

"Sure," he replied looking over at Clara. "I think we have enough wood and firelighters."

"Yes we do," added Clara looking back at Henry then Matthew.

"Can I help light it, Daddy?" asked Harriet.

"Of course, we'll get it going after we've all tidied up, and pitched the tent," he replied.

"Can I pitch the tent?" asked Matthew fidgeting in his chair.

"Uh, okay, we'll do it together," Henry replied.

So the chores were completed first, the children helping with the keenness they usually have when they want the next thing to start as soon as possible.

Matthew ran outside carrying the tent, and began to unravel the components, with Charlie and Sebastian following his lead. Clara supervised them, while Henry and Harriet collected some wood from the garage. Harriet carried the lightest bag of kindling to the fire-pit and began to tip it into the middle. The fire-pit was simple, a round charred bit of earth surrounded by six thick slices of tree trunk that were used as seats.

The four-person tent was pitched a couple metres away from the fire-pit. This, Matthew explained to the others, was to make sure of two things. First sparks from the fire would not catch the fabric, nor would the fabric get too hot and melt. Secondly the tent would not fill up with smoke or carbon monoxide, with potentially serious and life-threatening consequences. As Clara and Henry listened to Matthew's explanation during the tent's construction, they felt a sense of pride.

"Is that right, Mum?" Matthew asked now and then for reassurance.

"You're doing great darling, well done," she responded with a smile.

Henry arranged the kindling strategically in a pyramidal structure for maximum oxygen flow. He was explaining every step to Harriet who followed his instructions with care. Finally with bigger logs placed around the kindling, Harriet held the long lighter close to the firelighters in amongst the wood, with Henry's arm steadying and guiding it.

With the fire alight and the tent constructed, Clara left Henry with the children who were now all sitting round the fire with him. She returned a little while later with a tray of mugs of hot chocolate. The five of them were still sitting where she had left them. The fire had a warm hypnotic effect, and their eyes were glazed over with a blank look, as they stared at the dancing flames.

"Hot chocolate anyone?" she called out as she approached. Cries of yes please were followed by movement as, one by one, the children awoke from their dream and jumped up to pick up their warm chocolate drink. Clara sat next to Henry and handed him the last mug. Henry had proposed to her beside a campfire on a secluded Scottish beach many years before. It was an intimate and romantic setting with the sound of the ocean waves relentless but soothing.

Darkness fell around them and the background features of the garden blended into an inky blackness. As they sat talking, the yellow light from the fire illuminated their faces. The logs popped as the water inside them rapidly expanded turning into steam. Indiana was curled up between Clara and Henry.

"Dad – Aunt Jane told us a ghost story," Matthew exclaimed, excited by the recollection.

"Did she?" replied Henry.

Matthew enthusiastically recounted the tale. His working memory was perfect in every detail, and his wide eyes provided dramatic effect. Sebastian and Charlie punctuated his story with 'whoa' and gasps, as he continued.

"Wow, that's awesome," said Sebastian, as he finished.

"Have you seen a ghost, Daddy?" asked Harriet.

"No darling," replied Henry. "I've never seen one."

"I wonder what would've happened if the vicar wasn't there?" asked Charlie.

"Well, remember he said when you need it, help is never far away," Clara responded. "But there's no reason to worry around here, lovely," she said, to steer the conversation to a more cheerful place. The logs were now all burning steadily, the roaring flames had died down but the heat had intensified.

Charlie was enjoying the open fire, which only ever happened at Matthew's place. "Imagine," she said, "if we were sitting in my garden now and the lions roared - that would also be scary, huh?"

"Gosh yes!" responded Sebastian. Sebastian, with his thick unruly hair, was a curious boy. Always eager to explore, discover and figure things out. Sebastian did not like animals as much as Matthew, but they bonded, with a mutual respect of each other's intellect. Both picked things up quickly and enjoyed music and playing guitar.

"Right kids, we'll leave you out here for a bit - we'll be in the lounge if you need us." Henry got up. Clara followed his lead and reached for his hand. They walked back to the house, best friends together, hand in hand and chatting. Indiana followed them into the house, leaving the children alone.

"Did you hear anything back about the poachers?" Charlie asked Matthew.

"What poachers?" asked Sebastian looking between the two, puzzled.

"We found a deer leg," Harriet said, looking at him.

Matthew went onto repeat what the RSPCA inspector had said when they reported it. "The inspector was glad we'd brought it in. But if it was poachers, he didn't think they'd ever be caught."

"So - did he actually think it was a poacher?" asked Charlie.

"Yes, possibly - and he was going to take it to a vet for an opinion." Matthew replied.

"But Kings Wood is so big," shouted Harriet.

"And they probably hunt at night." Matthew continued; his eyes were wide open to emphasise his point.

"So they may never be caught?" asked Charlie, looking at Matthew.

"No," he sighed, "it's so unfair, those poor creatures," he added solemnly.

Matthew went onto add that the RSPCA inspector said that a lot of wild animals were being poached now. In the area, not only rabbits and pheasants were being stolen for food but also swans were disappearing.

"So what are they going to do?" Sebastian asked.

Matthew said that it was unlikely that any poachers would ever be caught. There was not much for the inspectors to go on. He said they had stepped up patrols in the area, but poachers usually waited until the dead of night to pick off unsuspecting deer. "It's terrible," he added.

Harriet needed the toilet and after announcing this to the three others, she got up and ran indoors.

"We should do something," Matthew said assertively.

"What can we do?" Sebastian said, sounding defeated.

"What if we could get more evidence and find the poachers?" Matthew asked.

"We'd have to go back at night," said Charlie, buying into Matthew's enthusiasm.

"We could camp in the woods," Matthew suggested.

"I could ask my Dad!" Sebastian offered. "He's said about camping out together, and it'll be my birthday soon – I'll ask if you could come along too."

"That's a great idea!" exclaimed Charlie.

"But I'm not sure my Dad would be happy to chase poachers in the night," added Sebastian. "It sounds a bit dangerous."

"Well, let's not mention it to him then," Charlie said looking at Matthew and Sebastian for agreement.

"But - we'll stick together with my Dad though?" asked Sebastian nervously.

"Yeah – sure we will," Matthew said to appease him and looking at Charlie to agree.

"Kids – come and wash your faces and get into your pyjamas now please!" Clara hollered from the patio door.

Charlie jumped up first. "I'll get there first!" she laughed, as she ran in.

The two boys jumped up simultaneously laughing and running.

"No you won't!" Matthew called.

The evening eventually ended with the four tucked in their sleeping bags and falling soundly asleep.

## *Chapter Seven*

**M**ark was the father of Sebastian. He often complained to his wife Harper about not getting out enough as a family, but Harper was not at all the outdoor type. She was afraid of most things that flew or buzzed around her. Her ideal weekend was spent visiting museums or art galleries and eating out in cafés or restaurants. When Sebastian had returned home from his sleepover and asked about the four of them spending the night camping in Kings Wood, he had agreed despite reservations about the location. Sebastian had talked many times about Matthew's adventures outdoors, up mountains or in the dark with his parents. Mark felt obliged to present himself too as an outdoor hero, which his son could look up to.

The reality is, of course, that you cannot be all things to all people. The trick is to find your niche and be good at it. That is what having friends is for after all. They offer diversity of experience. We cannot possibly all be the same. Friendships are built on mutual trust and empathy for one another. Sometimes you can find someone who shares your soul, and this becomes so much more than just what you do together.

Early evening just prior to sunset, Mark pulled his blue Land Rover into the Kings Wood carpark. Matthew insisted he knew a great spot to camp. It was a clearing among the trees and concealed from all the paths. The four of them had backpacks. Matthew borrowed his mother's medium-sized pack and lent his to Charlie, who was excited about the evening ahead. Matthew had pleaded with both parents to let him bring Indiana, but both had said no. They knew how unsettled Indiana was camping out and he would likely run off to chase deer.

When they reached the area, Mark was pleased it was exactly as Matthew had described. They walked through densely packed trees and left the path to emerge into the clearing. It was at least fifty square metres and surrounded on all sides by trees and shrubs. Mark had bought a two-person dome tent for himself and Sebastian to sleep in. Matthew also carried a light two-person tent, which his parents often carried to use on mountain tops. He and Charlie would stick together, ideal they thought, to allow them to sneak off after dark.

Keen to start looking for evidence, Charlie announced she needed a wee. Matthew insisted he would accompany her to a spot away from the tents where she could go undisturbed. Mark let them go, asking them not to be too long. Gleefully the two ran away from the campsite.

They slowed down when they were well away and began to wander along a path that twisted and turned through the trees. About twenty metres ahead a herd of deer was grazing peacefully. They stopped and remained silent and still, watching the deer with fascination and hoping that a clue might present itself. The sun was still golden and the beams long and shallow as they came down from the sky. The glare from the sun was hitting their eyes, so they moved as quietly as they could sideways to avoid it. They decided to crouch behind the trunk of a sweet chestnut tree beside them. Then, much to their surprise and delight, a tall white deer emerged from behind a bush, moving gracefully and slowly. It was much closer to them than the other deer. It seemed to glow in the golden light, an aura shining around its body as if magical. The two just stared unable to look away, a sense of awe and wonder filling their hearts. The white deer grazed undisturbed by their presence, and they watched for what felt like an eternity.

Eventually it disappeared again into the trees and Matthew and Charlie spoke to each other. They were acutely aware they had been gone for a while, so they started slowly putting one foot in front of the other, moving away from the tree. This time however, sharp senses of the other deer picked up the human movement and they immediately looked up and directly at the children on the path. The herd of deer, alarmed, skipped back in among the trees and were gone.

When the children arrived back at the campsite, Mark asked if they were okay. "Yeah, sorry," said Charlie. "I didn't like the first spot Matthew took me too."

"Yeah," added Matthew, "then I needed to take a leak too." He looked back at Charlie, who smiled back at him.

Matthew knew it was not right to lie, but he thought it unimportant to tell the truth in this instance and it might, he thought, only get them into unnecessary trouble. The last thing he wanted was to lose the opportunity they had ahead of them.

"Well, okay," Mark responded.

They all sat on the grass in front of their tents chatting. Mark had packed some self-heating cans of hot chocolate, which he handed out. The children loved the novelty of them. Mark repeated the instructions out loud that they dutifully carried out. In no time, they were drinking the warm chocolate milk.

"This is great," remarked Sebastian, smiling at his father, who looked pleased as punch.

"Yes, awesome," agreed both Charlie and Matthew together.

As time passed, the darkness came down around them, like a veil over their eyes. Mark had a single freestanding camp light that he switched on.

"Okay guys," he said, "let's tuck in now, so we can rise early and leave before too many walkers come, eh?" It was a rhetorical question. Although they had a secluded spot, Mark was still nervous about whether or not they should be camping there at all. But the delight and thankfulness of his son was, he felt, worth the risk.

Matthew hung his head torch from a loop in the middle of the tent interior. He and Charlie spread out their things which included crisps and chocolate ready for the night ahead. They got into their sleeping bags fully dressed. As Mark came over to check they were settled, he peered in to see their bodies cocooned in the sleeping bags. Satisfied by this, he bid them goodnight. The two listened in silence to the sound of Mark and Sebastian's tent being zipped up and the muffled sound of the two chatting as they too settled down for the night.

Whispering to each other, Matthew and Charlie agreed they would wait longer until they could be really sure nobody would hear them get up and leave their tent.

They dozed off. But then Matthew woke up and shook Charlie awake. Opening her eyes, he whispered that he thought it would be safe. Charlie sat up, as Matthew groped for his head torch. Switching on the light, Charlie quickly found hers and both slowly and carefully wriggled out of their bags so as to be as quiet as they could.

Matthew began unzipping the tent with the same care. Stepping out one followed by the other, they stood still listening for signs of noise coming from the other tent. Charlie and Matthew only heard the sound of deep breathing and light snores.

"Let's go this way," whispered Matthew to Charlie. Matthew kept the head torch in his hand so he could direct it away from the other tent. They did not want light or sound to wake the others. Once they had crept far enough away not to be worried any more, they both put on their head torches and continued on to the path they had found previously. They hoped to see the deer again and planned to switch off their lights and hide at the first sign of any potential poachers creeping about in the darkness.

An owl hooted in the distance. The light from the headtorches shone brightly, moving up and down with their bobbing heads as they walked. Reaching the spot where the deer had been, Charlie turned her head to look into the trees and the light swung round with her. She was startled. All that could be seen in the dark were a number of eyes shining brightly, glowing a shade of amber. The eyes looked like devils peering back from the shadows of hell. Matthew's gaze followed hers as she gasped at the sight, but Matthew knowing they were the eyes of deer hiding in the trees, reassured her. The light reflected from the deer's eyes, as they waited patiently for the two to pass.

"That's so weird," whispered Charlie. She had been clinging onto Matthew's arm, but on finding out the truth, she released her grip.

They turned onto another path heading in a different direction through the trees. As the trees closed in once more around them, the silence was broken only by the creaking of branches and rustle of leaves above.

Matthew was used to walking in darkness and unafraid of it. Charlie on the other hand had never walked in the woods at night but was thrilled by the adventure of it all. "This is quite exciting," she said. "Most people would think we were crazy doing this."

"Yeah," said Matthew. "But it's the same place at night as it is in the day – you just can't see so far."

"Maybe one day I'll be allowed to come with you on a mountain adventure," said Charlie smiling.

Matthew turned to look at her, forgetting his head torch would follow.

"Argh!" exclaimed Charlie, quickly covering her eyes. "You're blinding me!"

"Oh, sorry – I forgot," he said quickly looking away. "Come on, let's go a bit deeper." He walked off ahead.

Charlie continued, a step behind him, looking about with her light, this way and that. Then Matthew stopped, with Charlie bumping into him.

"I feel something strange," he said. He looked about but was unable to see anything. "I feel like..." He paused.

Charlie was looking from side to side and said quietly "like – we're being watched."

"You feel it too?" he asked, also talking more quietly now.

"Yes," she replied. "Shall we turn our head torches off?"

"Good idea," and Matthew's hand reached up and switched off his torch.

Charlie did the same and standing still, they continued looking about in silence. There was nothing. No other lights, no sound of movement on the ground. The waning moon was still shining brightly and as their eyes adjusted to the darkness, slithers of silvery moon beams just penetrated the canopy above.

"Hello!" a gruff, old-sounding voice said out of nowhere.

The two gasped in air as the voice startled them. Shaking and looking about quickly in all directions, they could see nothing. Matthew put his head torch back on and Charlie quickly copied him.

"Did you hear that?" he asked looking around and scared.

"Yes I did," Charlie replied anxiously, "Who's there?" she called out, her voice as shaky as her body.

No reply came.

"Let's get out of here," Matthew said turning and grabbing Charlie's hand.

She agreed and turned too. But just as they did a mist appeared a couple of metres ahead and as they neared, it grew colder, much colder. They stopped, and saw their every breath come out of their mouths as steam in the now freezing temperature. The mist ahead of them was new, they had not seen it on the way before. The mist started to grow bigger and glow in the light from their heads. It then started to move quickly, but there was no wind. It spread out sideways and then curled in and moved around them until they were surrounded. The two watched on, gripping each other's hand, frozen in fear, their eyes wide and now breathing fast and shallow.

Then without warning the mist formed the shape of a giant arm reaching quickly out with slender fingers on the end as if to grab them. They screamed and ducked away just out of its reach.

"Let's run!" Matthew screamed.

Gripping Charlie's hand tightly he pulled her so hard that she stumbled with the surprise. But she quickly steadied herself as they ran back through the cold mist.

"Where are you going?" asked the old gruff voice, and the mist formed a ball which thrust into Matthews back pushing him over onto the ground. Charlie went over with him, but got up first, and turned towards the mist.

"Let us pass!" she screamed at it.

All of a sudden, she was lifted up in the air and pushed backwards against a tree as if a big force had taken her. She landed on the ground, groaning, slightly winded and a bit sore from hitting the tree.

Matthew looked up and saw her. "Charlie," he cried out. He pushed himself up and turned to the mist. He opened his mouth to take a breath in but it was as if something heavy was sitting on his chest. A cold sensation came over him and he trembled with fear, unable to scream. Surely this was it, he would die here he thought. But Charlie sat up and crawled a little way towards him before getting up slowly and, bent over, she now grabbed his arm and pulled him towards her. As Matthew was moved off the spot where he stood, air rushed into his lungs and he panted as he breathed again, drawing the oxygen back in and relinquishing his sense of doom. They ran blindly in the opposite direction, both their hearts beating out of their chest. But in the darkness, they had no idea where they were heading. They stopped, the lactic acid building up in their muscles with the oxygen debt. Bending over to catch their breath, they looked back and the mist was almost upon them.

Then something else they were not expecting happened. The white deer appeared beside them. The deer had a pure white aura, which glowed brightly, dazzling in the darkness. It stood tall and powerful above them. A sense of calm and peace filled up their hearts. They felt strong again as it stood next them. Charlie stood looking in surprise. Her hair was ruffled and her clothes dirty from being on the ground.

"Can you help us?" she asked.

Looking into the white deer's eyes, Charlie saw a white fire raging behind them. She felt compelled to reach out her arm and touch it. She did so, slowly. It felt odd, it was warm and tingly. As Charlie drew her arm back, she looked down at her hand. She turned it over slowly and uncurled her fingers to reveal a white flame burning in her palm.

The flame flickered without causing pain, and she knew it was a gift that would burn and destroy the misty ghost. Her heart was filled with joy, and bravely she turned knowing now from a place deep within her what she needed to do.

Matthew watched on in wonder as Charlie reached out her hand and the flame extended beyond to the mist. As it touched the mist, it burned with vigour. A flash of white flames filled the forest around them, but the trees did not catch alight. The mist vanished with a growl and the two were left standing alone with the white deer beside them.

Matthew and Charlie hugged each other with joy. Matthew grabbed Charlie's hand to look at her palm. The fire was gone, and they both looked up at the deer as it stood silently. "It's going to take us back," Charlie said out loud.

"Yes," replied Matthew, "I thought that too."

The white deer steadily walked ahead. The two holding hands, followed on behind silently watching it as they went.

Back at the clearing, where they were camping the two moved ahead of the deer as it stopped. When they turned around to say goodbye, the white deer had already gone.

It had vanished, and they were left alone.

Silently they got back into their tent and sleeping bags. Matthew re-hung his head torch in the middle above them and Charlie turned hers off. Laying down, facing each other, they just stared into each other's eyes. A few minutes later, Charlie yawned.

"I'm tired now," she said.

"Yeah, me too," he replied and lifted up his hand to turn off the light.

"Will you still hold my hand though?" asked Charlie.

"Yes," Matthew said, laying back down and reaching over to find it.

They laid there, holding hands until they fell asleep. The peace that filled them from the white deer penetrated their souls and they slept soundly until morning. The shared experience had now bound them together in a new closeness that forms an unshakeable bond. A bond that extends beyond time and space.

## *Chapter Eight*

***T***he next morning, Mark and Sebastian were awake and chatting by six. Some days that begin in complete ordinariness can, for some, shape up to be extraordinary. This seemed like an ordinary late summer morning to Mark. Except for the fact he did not usually wake up in a woodland, Mark was not expecting anything unusual to take place. As he emerged from the tent, everything was exactly as he remembered the night before.

Matthew and Charlie's green tent was silent as they were still asleep. Mark walked over and unzipped their tent to look inside. The two were curled up inside their sleeping bags, Matthew's face was visible as he lay on his back, mouth open still fast asleep. The two had rolled apart as they had slipped into an unconscious state.

"Time to start waking up you two," Mark announced quietly at first into the tent. Nothing stirred, not even an eyelid twitched. "Hey, time to start waking up you two," Mark repeated a little louder.

Matthew twitched first, an arm raised up to his face and the back of his hand rubbed his nose. "Time to wake up," Mark repeated again, louder still as his patience waned. Matthew opened his eyes and blinked repeatedly as he started to focus on the shape by the tent door.

"Uh – um, okay," Matthew replied.

"Okay – don't go back to sleep now – time to pack away and have breakfast," Mark instructed. "Charlie – are you awake?" he asked.

"Hmm," replied Charlie.

"Well, that's great - get up now and pack up ready for breakfast," Mark said again, as Matthew sat up. Satisfied, Mark got up and walked away from them to start packing away himself.

Inside the tent Matthew put his hand on Charlie's shoulder and gently shook her until she rolled over to look at him. Her hair which had been perfectly brushed and put into pig tails was now sticking out in all directions. Parts of it looked like they had been back combed deliberately like that to give her a dishevelled look.

"Nice hair," Matthew chuckled as he looked at her.

"What!" Charlie said sitting upright. Bringing her hands to her head, she started to feel around her wildly tangled locks. "Oh," she said, as she pulled the bands off and attempted to smooth her hair back.

"Did that really happen last night?" Matthew asked watching her.

She looked back at him. "The white deer?" she said holding his gaze.

"Yes. Then it did happen. Wow, what are we going to say about it?" he asked.

"Well - why not everything?" she said excitedly. Her face lit up thinking about the magical experience of the white deer. The coldness and fear they had experienced before it had arrived was almost driven from her memory, until Matthew reminded her of it.

"Well – not everyone will be pleased about what that nasty ghost did to us," he said.

"You mean our parents?"

"Yeah – I think they might not be happy for us to go on more adventures, if they knew."

"But I want to tell everyone about the white deer – I mean it was so amazing – I couldn't keep that a secret!"

"No – no, of course not," Matthew agreed, "but maybe we should just say the ghost chased us and nothing else, that's all I meant."

"Yeah, okay – are you alright?" Charlie asked looking concerned.

"Of course, I just can't believe it happened. If you know what I mean?"

"Yeah, I get it, I asked for help, and it told me to take the fire from its eye's," Charlie's eyes glazed over in wonder.

"Amazing," Matthew said, still watching Charlie.

"I had fire in my hand!" Charlie exclaimed, with wide eyes.

"Is it scarred?" Matthew said reaching out. Charlie gave him her hand and they both looked as she opened her palm and turned it over. "Not a single mark on it," he whispered looking astounded.

"Are you up yet, you two?" the voice of Mark called from outside.

"Yes we are," Matthew and Charlie replied, almost simultaneously.

"Great, get packed up then," Mark responded with an edge to his voice that suggested they should do this quickly.

They began stuffing the contents of the tent into their bags. Unzipping the tent and stepping out, both were grinning with joy, as they busily set about dismantling the tent.

The morning was bright with a shining sun, but thick billowy clouds were dotted randomly in the western part of the sky. If you had been there observing this scene, you would not have had a clue about what had occurred the night before. It is impossible to judge correctly what has gone on or is inside a person until a story is revealed. Until we know for sure, our minds simply fill in the gaps for us, but often incorrectly.

"Hey guys," Sebastian called merrily as he wriggled out of his tent, with his backpack, shunted in front of him. As he stood up, he noticed the dirtiness of Matthew and Charlies' clothes.

"Hey," they both responded, as they turned to look at him.

"You'll never guess what happened to us last night!" Charlie said quickly and with glee.

"What happened?" Sebastian asked.

Mark who was on his knees repacking his rucksack stopped to look up at Charlie.

"We went out to look for poachers and found a ghost and a magical white deer," she said quickly.

Mark and Sebastian looked confused and a little taken aback by the information.

"Oh my!" Charlie shouted. Her arms stretched out to her sides as if to hold onto something not there and her eyes looked downwards but vacant as she exclaimed again "Oh my – I know something!" Looking up, her eyes jumped between the other three as they stared back waiting expectantly for her to reveal more. "I know where the poacher is!"

"What poacher? What are you talking about?" Mark asked concerned. "And as for a magic deer, well I've heard of the white deer in Kings Wood – so I reckon you just saw something ordinary and are making up a story."

Sebastian shuffled uncomfortably wondering if they were about to get into some sort of trouble. He wondered if their plan to find this poacher would come out and his father would think he had been misled.

"We found a deer hoof," Matthew said looking directly at Mark.

"I know where we're going to find the answers – a little way up further in the woods," said Charlie.

All three still looked puzzled, so Charlie added that she didn't know how she knew, but just that somehow she knew and that they were meant to take a look.

"Now hang on a minute," Mark stood up, "I'm not sure what you are talking about but we're packing up to get out of here before anyone finds that we've been camping."

"If we're packed up, will it matter if anyone sees us?" Matthew asked.

"I suppose not," Mark replied. "Now I have no idea what you two have been up to..."

"But we can take a look Dad, can't we? What if there is a poacher and animals are being hurt?" Sebastian interrupted with a pleading tone.

"I suppose we can take a look if it's not far from here," Mark replied looking at his son and after a long pause he went on. "Now if we're staying a bit longer, we need to pack up quicker," he said with the edgy tone back in his voice.

At once the children started taking down the tent and packing. By six forty-five they had eaten and were ready to set off from the clearing.

"How do you know where we're going?" Sebastian asked.

"Like I said - I don't know - I just know. It must be that the white deer told me last night."

"You saw the white deer too?" Sebastian asked looking at Matthew.

"I did," Matthew nodded.

"What was it like? Did it have pink eyes? What about the ghost? Did you really see another ghost?" Sebastian persisted one question after another.

"I'll be telling your parents later about all this," Mark interjected before Charlie and Matthew could respond. "I'm sure they'll be very interested in you sneaking off out of the tent in the night," he added clearly annoyed that this had occurred on his watch.

"We didn't head out far," Matthew responded, trying to diffuse Mark's irritated mood.

The four emerged out of the trees and onto a large open bridleway. They travelled along the path which was long and mildly undulating. They had been walking fifteen minutes, when Mark reminded Charlie that she had said that their destination was close to the campsite.

"I don't think it's much further," she replied hopefully.

They crossed a large open junction which had forestry operations signs here and there. A small tractor could be seen amongst the trees. Just beyond that they passed a chipper and tall piles of logs with signs that warned people not to climb on the unstable structures.

The sunlight was becoming more diffuse as the cloud silently thickened above them. The forest sounds were tranquil, filled with the beauty of nature going about its morning routine, the chirping of birds, the gentle breeze moving through the trees. They had not come across any other people, but they could hear the sound of traffic in the distance becoming stronger.

Up ahead the path started to curve to the right. As they came around the bend a long straight stretch opened up with tall trees lining each side.

"I've been along here before," said Matthew. "There's a wooden hut a bit further up there. I've seen the tractors drive up to it."

"That's where I think we're meant to go," added Charlie, looking at Matthew first then to Mark and Sebastian.

"Okay – well it can't be far now then," Mark said. "Keep your eyes open and let's walk quietly."

As they drew near they could see a large black Land Rover parked to the side of the hut. Out the front of the hut Mark spotted a rifle left leaning up against the wall. "I don't like the look of this," he said.

"We should hide!" Matthew said quietly.

"Over there – look – we can hide there." Sebastian pointed off the path to the right. A tall pile of logs sat in the trees, close enough to keep watch on the hut but far enough away that they could whisper quietly to each other and not be heard.

They all crouched behind the logs. Mark insisted they would leave soon if nothing happened quickly. He looked again at the rifle and he could see a long black cylinder attached to the end of it. A silencer he thought. Only a poacher would need one of those in the woods. Sitting back behind the logs Mark could hardly believe that Charlie had been right in saying she knew where they would find clues. Mark was a strong believer in fate, and he reluctantly accepted that something had to be done. But the presence of a gun meant direct action was not a safe option.

"Dad - look - there's a man," whispered Sebastian anxiously.

All four peered around the edge of the logs, two at each end. They watched the man who was wearing all black except for an army style camouflage jacket. He picked up the rifle and walked to the back of the Land Rover. He appeared to be packing up. It was then that they realised there was a deer carcass on the ground on the other side of the Rover.

Mark got out his phone and used the camera to zoom in and take a few pictures of the scene. Sitting back behind the logs he reviewed the photographs and realised that he had the number plate of the vehicle. Mark decided that they would leave and head back into town and report what they had seen. With no signal where they were in the woods, they did not have any other option.

The man in the jacket went about his illegal business completely unaware he was being watched from a distance. He had the deer carcass on a plastic sheet and they watched as he dragged it along to the back of the vehicle.

"Right, he's busy probably getting that deer into the back. It's time we left!" Mark instructed the children to go directly backwards from behind the logs to give them cover, rather than head left and straight onto the path and risk being seen.

Quietly, the four bent over and tip toed across the ground away from the logs. After about fifty metres, they rejoined the path, straightened up and walked at speed in the direction of the carpark.

The sky had grown dark while they had been observing the poacher, and big drops of rain started to fall randomly around them. Then there was a rumble in the distance.

"It's a thunderstorm!" Matthew shouted as they began trotting as fast as they could.

"That can't be good," Mark added. "Come on keep moving quickly," he encouraged them nervously. The rain became heavy and it was hard to look ahead without being pelted hard in the face.

"Are the woods safe in a thunderstorm?" Charlie asked shouting over the din of the rain.

"Probably not," Matthew replied loudly.

"A car is the safest place to be isn't Dad?" asked Sebastian trying to look over at his father.

"Yes, that's right son - the car acts as a Faraday cage," he hollered.

"What's that?" asked Charlie.

"It just means the lightening would go around the outside of the vehicle if it was hit - leaving the people inside it safe."

"Oh, wow!" Charlie exclaimed, excited by the new knowledge. "We'd better hurry then!" she said as they all saw a flash.

Matthew started counting out loud. One one thousand, two one thousand, three one thousand... and a big bang boomed overhead. "It's close!" he exclaimed.

"What's the counting for?" Charlie asked still shouting.

"My Mum does it every time there's a storm – the number between the flash and the bang tells you how close the storm is."

"Is that because light travels faster than sound?" Sebastian added.

"Yeah, I guess," replied Matthew.

"Oh wow – I'd never thought of it like that – I'm going to count next time too," said Charlie still full of enthusiasm, despite being soaked through.

"Come on kids – this isn't a science lesson, we need to hurry up," Mark said impatiently and spitting water out as he spoke.

All four arrived back at the Land Rover soaked to the bone. Though it was still early, a couple of other vehicles had already parked, and dogs and owners were rushing back for shelter.

Inside the Rover Mark wiped his face and started the engine to get the heater going. "Is everyone okay?" he asked looking around. Replies from all his passengers were positive, and they were eager for him to check and see if his phone had regained a signal. It had not - but Mark was content to drive to the police station. When everyone was belted in, he set off.

## *Chapter Nine*

**M**ark turned left out of the car park to head down the hill towards the main road. In no time they had passed the second smaller car park, empty of vehicles. Mark took a deep breath as he shrugged his shoulders and settled into the driver's seat. Glad to be back in the comfort of his Land Rover, he had a momentary sense of feeling back in control of events.

Then from nowhere the black Land Rover they had seen with the poacher emerged just ahead of them from a forest track.

"Oh my goodness!" Mark exclaimed. "It's the guy!"

"Oh - follow him Dad!" Sebastian cried out excitedly.

Charlie and Matthew were in agreement and just as excited.

"Keep calm, keep calm," Mark said out loud but to himself as much as the others. "You see people on TV doing this sort of thing, but not me."

"Are you going to follow him Dad?" Sebastian asked after listening to his father's murmurs.

"Yes - I am aren't I?" he retorted defensively but feeling slightly anxious.

The children chatted excitedly; where was he going? How many deer did he have in the back? Could they call the police to join in the chase? As they approached a junction ahead the poacher indicated right, and Mark did the same. It didn't take long for the black Rover to turn and after looking both ways, Mark did the same. Fortunately he thought, this was the way he had intended to go. The poacher accelerated quickly and was soon racing off at sixty miles per hour on a straight stretch of road.

"He's getting away," Sebastian cried out worried they would lose him.

"I can see that," Mark replied, "but I don't want to look like I'm tailing him. He might get suspicious."

"He didn't see us in the woods, so he can't think we're onto him," said Matthew.

"Yeah," Charlie agreed.

"I know, I know - but I just want to take it steady, not look out of the ordinary," explained Mark.

Mark did his best to catch up a bit without going over the speed limit. He kept the black vehicle just in his sights ahead. As they came into the town, other traffic slowed the pursuit and as the poacher took the third exit off a roundabout, Mark had to stop to let other cars through from his right.

Now two cars behind the poacher, Mark was confident that he would never suspect they were following him.

"Shall we call the police now?" Charlie asked.

"Err, no – we'll just see where he goes first and then we'll be able to give them a bit more information."

"This is so cool Dad!" Sebastian said grinning and the others agreed.

Then the poacher turned into a side street behind a row of shops and restaurants. Mark and the children saw where he went, but Mark continued on without turning. Matthew, Charlie and Sebastian rotated a hundred and eighty degrees to look back.

"He's parked up outside a garage," Charlie said with a breathy excitement.

"Right! Now we'll head onto the police station – I know the name of that street."

Arriving at the station all four were taken into an interview room. They left drips and wet footprints on the polished floors on the way. A superintendent took a statement from Mark and also wrote the names and addresses of Matthew and Charlie in case they needed to come back for more information.

Charlie didn't explain about the white deer. They just said they were exploring. Who would believe them if they started talking about ghosts and white flames? The officer asked Mark if he would like to be kept up to date with any developments in the case and he said he would.

"You've done a good thing. It's not often people get caught in the act of catching and killing wild animals, and with a firearm. It's sounds like we might get this one," said the officer as they all stood up. Mark shook hands with the officer and they left.

Mark called home before heading back. Harper was concerned. The children heard Mark giving repeated assurances that they were all safe and that although it sounded risky, they were never really in any danger. It appeared to Matthew that Mark was quite enjoying the tale. He was playing the reluctant hero of the hour.

Sebastian was pleased that they had solved the mystery of the deer hoof. All of them felt a deep satisfaction that the mission had been accomplished. The slaughter would cease, and the deer would live in harmony with nature once more. During the long drive back, Matthew and Charlie messaged their parents with an estimated time to pick them up from Sebastian's house.

The tale was told over again to all the parents, and the speculation as to what might happen to the poacher was discussed. Rosie thought the police might have to put the poacher's place under surveillance to make sure it was safe before officers could go in. Clara and Henry arrived together with Harriet and they thought armed officers would surround the place and enter under the cover of darkness.

All of them that agreed they would be keeping a close eye on the news, and Clara set up a tweet alert from the Kent police account to monitor events. They were all very sure something would happen and quite quickly.

Later, Charlie and Matthew told their tale of the ghost and the white deer. Both could have regretted leaving the tent. They could have been traumatised by their night, but neither of them felt that way. If it had not been for the nasty ghost, then they felt sure that the miracle of the white deer would not have taken place. Then of course, Charlie would not have known the location of the poacher. Something very good came out of what had initially seemed bad.

Difficult experiences can shape young hearts and minds by stealing their joy. But on the other-hand, they can just as much develop resilience and strengthen a character to cope better with the inevitable ups and downs that the journey of life entails. Charlie and Matthew chose to focus on the good, and in their hearts remembered the light overcoming the darkness. Both Charlie and Matthew slipped back easily into the normality of daily life.

~

Ten days after the events of their adventure in the woods, Rosie came over to see Clara for a cup of tea and chat. On arrival Charlie whizzed off upstairs with Matthew and Clara put the kettle on. Clara and Rosie discussed the events that followed. The police had arrested the poacher after an armed raid. It turned out the poacher was a celebrated local chef and restaurant owner. His friends and neighbours suggested that he had been under pressure and desperate to cut costs and increase business by any means. His permit to hold a firearm was out of date and this would increase the likelihood of a prison sentence. The local papers reported that police and RSPCA inspectors found evidence that he had not only been taking deer, but also rabbit, pheasant and possibly swan. They were waiting for the results of DNA analysis for confirmation.

Mark had been contacted by local reporters after his part in the drama was revealed. His photograph was published as the hero who stumbled upon the crime in the woods. They were offered free meals at local restaurants as a reward. Both Harper and Mark talked about the events to friends, family and even strangers coming up to them during shopping trips on the high street or in supermarkets. Their fame locally was a passing excitement that they both revelled in.

As Clara and Rosie chatted about the events, Harriet who had been watching television, wandered out of the lounge and into the kitchen.

"I'm hungry," she announced. After agreeing a sandwich would fill the void in her stomach, Clara asked her to head upstairs and see if Matthew and Charlie wanted something to eat too.

Harriet dutifully ran upstairs and burst into Matthew's room. Charlie and Matthew were jumping up and down dancing to the music playing through Alexa. Harriet loved talking to Alexa and before remembering her task, she shouted at the device to turn the lights on and then to change from white to red. The device did as it was told and a red glow filled the room. Matthew and Charlie were laughing as they continued throwing themselves around and Harriet jumped on the bed and started bouncing up and down.

Remembering she was hungry, she commanded "Alexa stop the music," and at once it shut off.

"Hey!" Matthew shouted annoyed.

"Mum wants to know if you want to eat now."

"Oh - okay, yeah," and Matthew left the room. He ran down the stairs, with Harriet and Charlie following on behind.

As they all landed out of breath and giggling in the kitchen, Clara and Rosie wanted to know what they had been up to. Charlie and Harriet explained simultaneously, while Matthew peered over his mother's arm to look at the sandwich she was preparing.

"Can I get you something to eat?" Clara asked looking both at Rosie and Charlie.

"No thanks, lovely," replied Rosie, "we had better set off. Thank you for the cup of tea, but we'll head back and have dinner. Phil will be back soon."

Charlie looked sullen, and her shoulders dropped as they moved towards the door. Clara and Rosie both chuckled at the long face. "You'll see each other again soon enough!" said Rosie.

"Inseparable now these two eh?" Clara commented with a smile and raised eyebrows.

Clara and Rosie had a momentary embrace as they said goodbye. When the front door closed, Matthew asked for a ham and cheese sandwich.

"Okay darling – then shall we put a film onto watch before your Dad gets home?"

Both Harriet and Matthew thought that was a great idea and they quickly settled on watching "The Last Jedi."

As she made the sandwiches, Clara remarked what an interesting summer it had been with many adventures.

"Yes - but I want to see the white deer," Harriet blurted.

"Me too," remarked Clara smiling. "You have plenty to tell your grandparents when they arrive to stay this weekend."

"Yay!" Harriet said with a little jump up and down.

With the food prepared, Clara carried the two plates into the lounge. The children ran to get a seat on the sofa. Matthew pulled a blanket over their legs, and each then took a plate from their mother. After returning to the kitchen for drinks, Clara came back and started the DVD. She joined the two children who eventually snuggled on either side of her, after eating all they wanted.

Indiana, who had been sniffing around the garden, wandered slowly back in, licked each plate left on the floor, mopping up the leftover bits of crust, and laid down at Clara's feet. They watched him and chuckled. He never missed a trick when it came to food.

It had been a long summer of adventure, but now in this moment they were content to rest and be at peace in the place they called home.

www.ingramcontent.com/pod-product-compliance
Lightning Source LLC
LaVergne TN
LVHW010455160826
845677LV00012B/2495